Grimm's
fairy tales

Illustrated By
Greg Hildebrandt

The Unicorn Publishing House, Inc.
New Jersey

Sleeping Beauty

There once lived a King and a Queen, who were childless. They had always wanted a child, but for a long time had none. Then one day, they happened upon a frog, who said, "Within one year, you shall have a child." And at the end of a year, a beautiful daughter was born.

The King called for a royal feast to be held. And what a grand feast it was. It seemed everyone in the kingdom was invited. Even the fairies were invited, that is, all except one. There was one fairy who was most wicked, and the King prayed she would not hear of the feast. But she did.

She appeared in a terrible rage, for in truth, she was angry and hurt that she was not invited. She placed a horrible curse upon the poor child, crying out, "When the Princess reaches her fifteenth birthday she shall prick herself on a spinning wheel and fall dead!" Without another word, the fairy vanished.

Everyone was horrified, but another fairy quickly stepped forward, saying, "Though I cannot break this wicked curse, I can soften it. The Princess shall not die, but will fall into a deep sleep that will last a hundred years."

The King was so fearful for his daughter's safety that he ordered all the spinning wheels in the kingdom to be gathered up and burned. As time went on, the Princess grew into a beautiful and thoughtful young woman.

Now it happened that on her fifteen birthday the King and Queen were away from home, leaving the Princess quite alone. She decided to take a walk through the castle that morning, and in a little room she found an old woman, busily working on a spinning wheel. "Good day, Granny," said the Princess. "What are you doing?"

"I am spinning, my child."

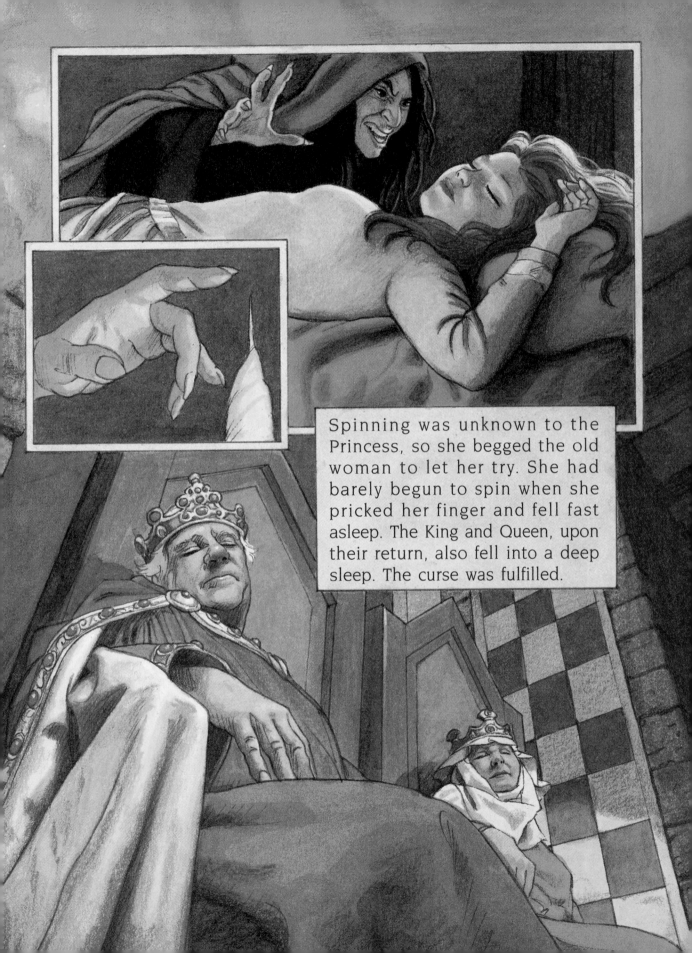

Spinning was unknown to the Princess, so she begged the old woman to let her try. She had barely begun to spin when she pricked her finger and fell fast asleep. The King and Queen, upon their return, also fell into a deep sleep. The curse was fulfilled.

In fact, everyone in the castle fell fast asleep. The evil fairy then cast a wicked spell and a huge hedge of briar roses grew up around the castle. The briars grew so high that they surrounded the castle like a fortess wall. As long as the Princess lay asleep, all were forbidden to enter lest the curse be broken.

But many tried—*and many failed*. The legend grew up in the land that there was a lovely Sleeping Beauty, Briar Rose, within the castle walls. Knights came from far and wide to try to rescue her. All soon found themselves lost or trapped in the briar hedge and died miserable deaths.

After many years had passed a young Prince came
to the kingdom and heard the story of Sleeping
Beauty. He determined he would try to save her.
Now luckily, on the day he entered the briar hedge
a hundred years had passed, and the Princess was
to wake up that very morning. The hedge opened
up before him as he made his way to the castle.

He entered the castle and found the King and Queen asleep on their thrones. The Prince searched throughout the castle, where he found the cook, the maids, and even the Princess' pet doves all fast asleep. At last he reached the room where the Princess was asleep.

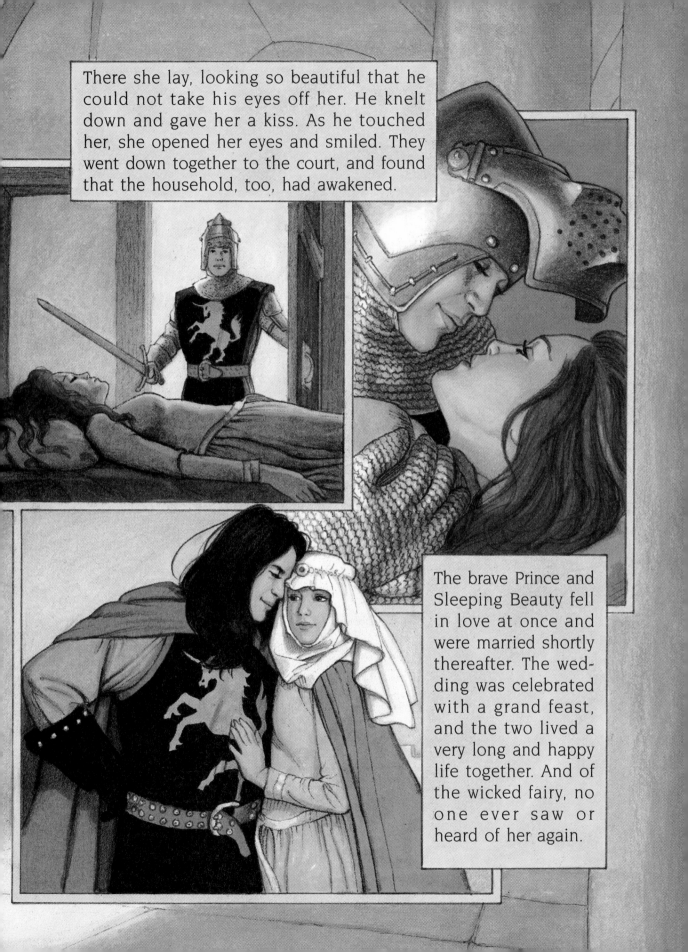

There she lay, looking so beautiful that he could not take his eyes off her. He knelt down and gave her a kiss. As he touched her, she opened her eyes and smiled. They went down together to the court, and found that the household, too, had awakened.

The brave Prince and Sleeping Beauty fell in love at once and were married shortly thereafter. The wedding was celebrated with a grand feast, and the two lived a very long and happy life together. And of the wicked fairy, no one ever saw or heard of her again.

Rumpelstiltskin

There was once a poor miller who loved to boast. Now this miller had a beautiful daughter, and it happened one day that he spoke to the King. He lied, saying, "Sire, I have a daughter who can spin gold out of straw."

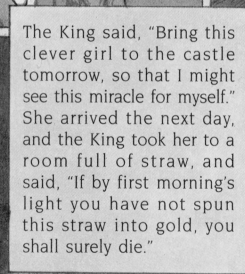

The King said, "Bring this clever girl to the castle tomorrow, so that I might see this miracle for myself." She arrived the next day, and the King took her to a room full of straw, and said, "If by first morning's light you have not spun this straw into gold, you shall surely die."

The poor girl sat and began to sob, for she didn't have the least idea of how to spin straw into gold. All at once there appeared a little man, who said, "Do not weep my child, for I can spin straw into gold! But if I do, what will you give me in return?"

"I will give you my necklace," she said, smiling. Taking the necklace, he sat down to his work.

He worked all night at the spinning wheel, and to the girl's
amazement and delight, he
indeed spun straw into gold.
Just before morning he finished
his magical work. With all the
straw now spun into gold, he
bid the girl good-day and left.

When the King returned that morning, he was delighted by the sight of a room full of gold. But he was not yet satisfied. He took the girl to a still larger room full of straw, and said, "If you value your life, spin this straw into gold by first morning's light, or you shall die." After the King left, she began to weep. But again the little man appeared.

"What will you give me if I spin the straw into gold for you?" he asked.
"I will give you the ring off my finger."
The little man agreed, and taking the ring, sat down and spun all the straw into gold.

The King was amazed to find another room full of gold. He took her quickly to a huge room full of straw, and said, "This last room of straw you must spin into gold in one night, but if you do you shall be my Queen and rule the whole kingdom by my side."

When she was alone the little man came again to her, saying, "If I spin the straw into gold, what will you give to me?"
"I have nothing left that I can give."

"Well then, you must promise me your first child if you become Queen! If you will promise me that, I will spin the straw into gold."

The girl thought it a silly demand and decided to promise the little man what he wanted, knowing full well she would never keep such a promise. The little man was satisfied, though, and spun the straw into gold.

The King *did* keep his promise, and married the miller's daughter at once. She became a Queen.

When a year had passed a daughter was born. The Queen had forgotten all about her promise to the little man. But he appeared one day before her at the castle.

"I have come for the child. Give her to me as you promised."
The Queen began to weep and moan so that the little man finally said, "I will give you three days, and if you can tell me my name within that time you can keep the child."
Then he left her.

When he came the next day, she tried every name she could think of, but every time he replied, "No, no, no, that's not my name. You now have but two days to guess my name."

The Queen sent her servants throughout the kingdom to find out who the little man was, but no one seemed to know him. "No, no, no, that's not my name. You have but one day for this guessing game."

The third day a servant returned, saying, "I found a little man last night singing by a fire deep in the woods. He sang, 'Today I bake and brew my beer./Tomorrow I bring the Queen's child here./Oh! lucky for me not a soul does know/That Rumpelstiltskin is my name. Ho! Ho!'" The Queen cried with joy upon hearing the name.

The little man arrived soon after, and the Queen politely asked, "Is your name Tom? No? Is it Harry? No? Is it Joseph? No?" And then with a little smile, she said, "Is it, by chance, Rumpelstiltskin?"

"The devil told you that! The devil told you that!" he screamed. "Unfair! Unfair!" And in a rage he stamped one foot down, then the other, and then both feet, till he went right through the floor and disappeared underground forever.

Snow-White & Rose-Red

Once there was a poor widow who lived in a little hut with her two daughters. One girl was named Snow-White and the other was called Rose-Red, as they had been named after the flowers that grew around the cottage. They loved each other dearly and never parted.

Now it happened one cold and snowy winter night, a knock came at the door. Rose-Red opened the door, thinking it was some traveler needing shelter. She froze with fright at the sight of a huge bear.

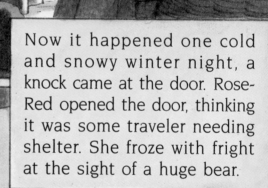

The bear, however, spoke gently to her, saying, "Don't be afraid, I will not harm you. I am frozen and only wish to come in and warm myself." She led him to the warm fire and the two girls brushed the snow from his frosty coat.

From that night on they became the best of friends. The bear would often visit them, spending the night by the warm fire. But with the coming of spring, the bear said to them, "I must go away, and I cannot return the whole summer." Sadly, the girls waved good-bye."

One spring day, as the girls gathered wood in the forest, they came across a dwarf, who had caught his beard in a split tree. "What have you done to yourself, little man?" asked Snow-White.

"Foolish child!" said he. "Can't you see I caught my beard while splitting this log. Here it sticks and I cannot get away. Help me!" The girls thought hard of what to do.

They tried hard to pull the little man free, but his beard was caught too tightly in the log. "Ouch! You cruel girls! You're killing me! Ouch!"

Then Rose-Red had an idea. She took a little knife and cut his beard free. "Stupid child! Oh, my beautiful beard! Curse you for your foolishness!" And the dwarf grabbed his sack of gold and left without one word of thanks.

Some weeks later they came across the dwarf again, this time with his beard caught in a fishing line. "Oh, don't just stand there fools, help me before the fish pulls me into the water!" he cried with rage.

Rose-Red took her knife out and clipped his beard free once more. "No, no! What have you done, you dumb child! My lovely beard! Gone! Gone!" Taking up a sack of pearls, he left all in a huff.

Not many days after, they saw the rude little man again in the forest. As he walked along, a giant eagle swooped down and grabbed him up. The girls ran to him at once and held tight to his legs lest he be carried away and eaten. The eagle struggled to lift the dwarf, but at last it released its grip and the little man came tumbling down to the ground.

He should have been thankful to the girls for saving his life, but the ungrateful dwarf only screamed, "Could you not have treated me more gently? Look! my coat is torn! You are both meddling fools!" And he threw a sack of precious stones over his shoulder and left without another word.

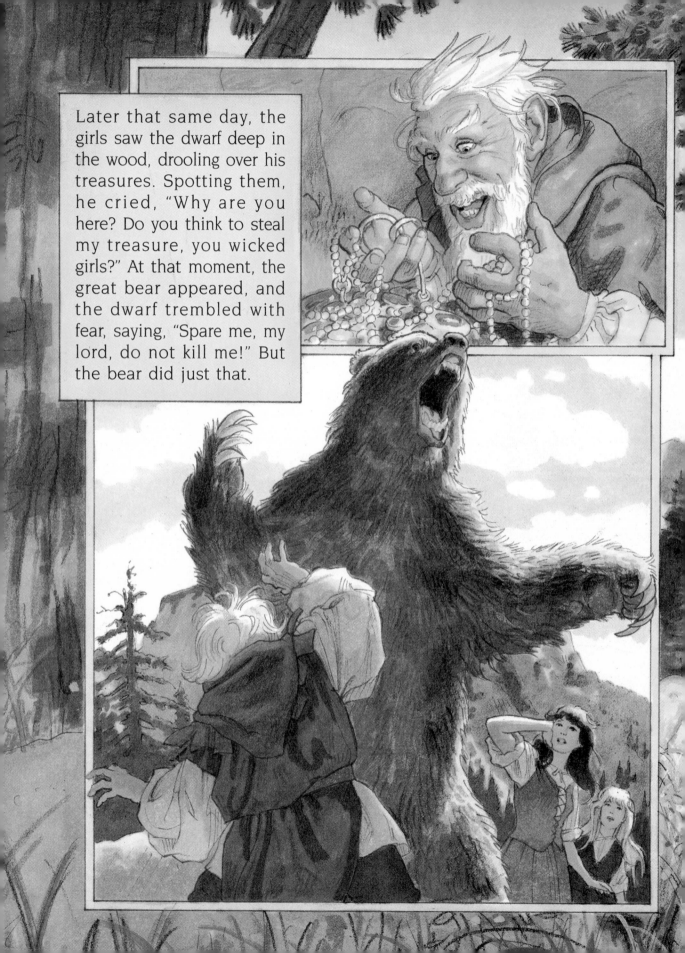

Later that same day, the girls saw the dwarf deep in the wood, drooling over his treasures. Spotting them, he cried, "Why are you here? Do you think to steal my treasure, you wicked girls?" At that moment, the great bear appeared, and the dwarf trembled with fear, saying, "Spare me, my lord, do not kill me!" But the bear did just that.

The girls stood amazed as they saw the furry coat of the bear fall off, and a handsome prince now stood before them, and said, "Do not fear, for you see, that wicked dwarf cast a spell on me to steal my riches." And the three hugged, and were dear friends for life.

Red Riding Hood

Once upon a time there was a sweet little girl whom everybody loved. But most of all, she was loved by her grandmother. She had once given the little girl a red velvet cloak. The little girl loved it so much she would never wear anything else. And that is how she became known as Little Red Riding Hood.

One day her mother called to her, "Take these jellies and jams to Grandmother. She is not feeling well, and they will cheer her. And when you get there, don't forget to say 'Good morning,' and to be very polite."

Now her grandmother lived far in the woods, so Red Riding Hood set off at once. It wasn't long, though, before she met a Wolf. Red Riding Hood didn't know what a wicked fellow he was, so, of course, she wasn't a bit afraid.

"Good morning, Red Riding Hood," the Wolf said prettily.

"Good morning, Wolf," Red Riding Hood said.

"May I walk with you?" asked the Wolf. "Where are you off to, my child?"
"Come, walk with me, Wolf, for I am going to my grandmother's house far in the woods."
They walked together for a while when the Wolf had the wicked idea he would go ahead of her and eat the Grandmother, then wait for Red Riding Hood to come later and gobble her up also. He told the little girl she should pick pretty flowers as a present.

While the little girl picked pretty flowers in a field, the Wolf snuck off and made straightaway for the Grandmother's house. He knocked at the door, and he heard a voice say, "Red Riding Hood? Come, come in, my child."

He entered the cottage and ate the Grandmother up. Then he put some of her bedclothes on and climbed into bed to wait for Red Riding Hood. When the little girl had picked enough flowers, she set off again for her Grandmother's house. Once there, she found the door wide open.

She went inside, and said, "Good morning, Grandmother." But she heard no reply. Coming closer, she said, "Oh, Grandmother, what big ears you have." "The better to hear you with, my dear."

"Grandmother, what big eyes you have," she said.
"The better to see you with, my dear," said the Wolf.
"What big hands you have, Grandmother."
"The better to catch hold of you with, my dear," said the Wolf, moving a bit closer.

"But Grandmother, what big teeth you have."
"The better to eat you up with, my dear."
Hardly had the Wolf said this than he jumped out of bed and swallowed poor Little Red Riding Hood up in one bite. Now the Wolf was very satisfied indeed, being so full, so he went back to the bed and laid down. Soon he was snoring loudly.

A hunter came passing by the Grandmother's house and stopped. "How loudly the old woman is snoring," he thought. "I should go and see if she is in any trouble.

Climbing up the hill to the house, the noble hunter knocked at the door, but he received no reply.

He entered quietly, and finding no one in the room, made his way to the bed. The bed curtains were drawn, but the deafening sound of snoring could be heard.

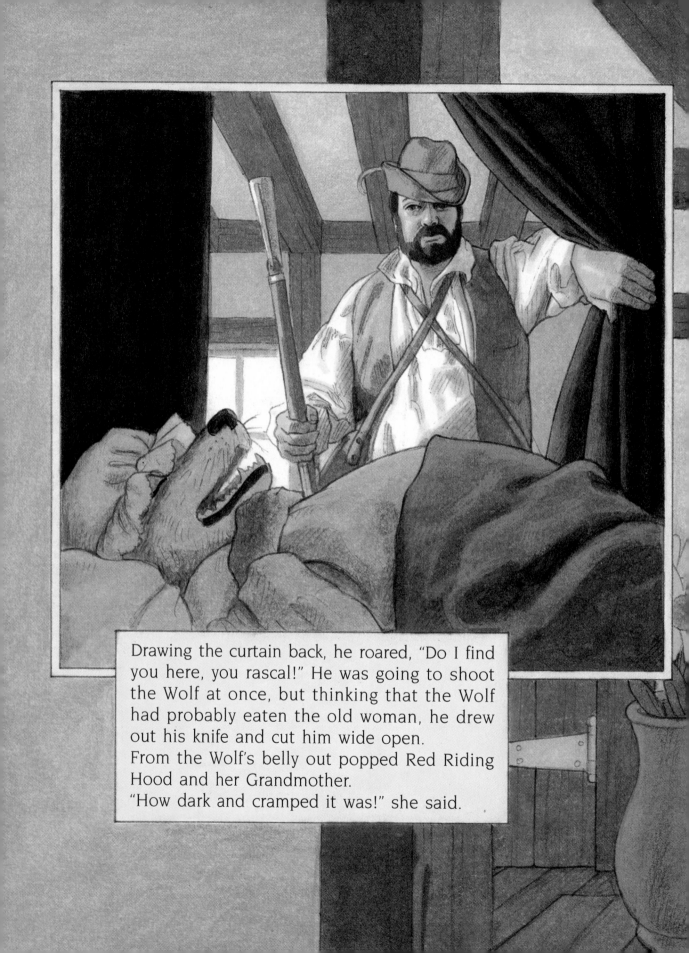

Drawing the curtain back, he roared, "Do I find you here, you rascal!" He was going to shoot the Wolf at once, but thinking that the Wolf had probably eaten the old woman, he drew out his knife and cut him wide open.
From the Wolf's belly out popped Red Riding Hood and her Grandmother.
"How dark and cramped it was!" she said.

The hunter took the dead wolf away and Red Riding Hood finally had her visit with her Grandmother. They ate cake and cookies and had a very happy time together. On her way back home, Red Riding Hood thought to herself, "I will never again wander off into the woods by myself, and never, oh never, will I talk to a Wolf!"

The
End

Brothers Grimm

Fairy Tales

Brothers Grimm

fairy tales

Illustrated By
Greg Hildebrandt

The Unicorn Publishing House, Inc.
New Jersey

Snow-White and the Seven Dwarfs

Once upon a time there was a beautiful but wicked Queen. She had a magic mirror, and she would stand before it and say, "Mirror, mirror on the wall,/Who is the fairest of them all?" And the mirror would answer, "You are fairest of them all." But one day when the Queen asked, the mirror said:

"Queen, you are full fair, 'tis true,/But young Snow-White is fairer than you." Snow-White was her step-daughter, and had now grown into a beautiful and gentle young woman.

The Queen was furious. From that moment on her heart turned to hatred against Snow-White. She called for a huntsmen, and told him to take Snow-White into the woods and put her to death.

But the hunter took pity on her and said, "I will not kill you, poor child. Leave here and never return again!"

Snow-White fled deep into the wild woods. She was in terror at every turn, but she didn't not know what to do except to go deeper and deeper into the forest. In the heart of the wood she came upon a tiny cottage.

Tired and hungry, she decided to go inside to rest. She found no one was at home, so she helped herself to a bit of bread and drink, and then laid down on a tiny bed and soon fell fast asleep.

It was quite dark when the little men came home. They were seven dwarfs who dug for gold in the mountains. Finding Snow-White asleep, they decided to let the poor child rest until morning.

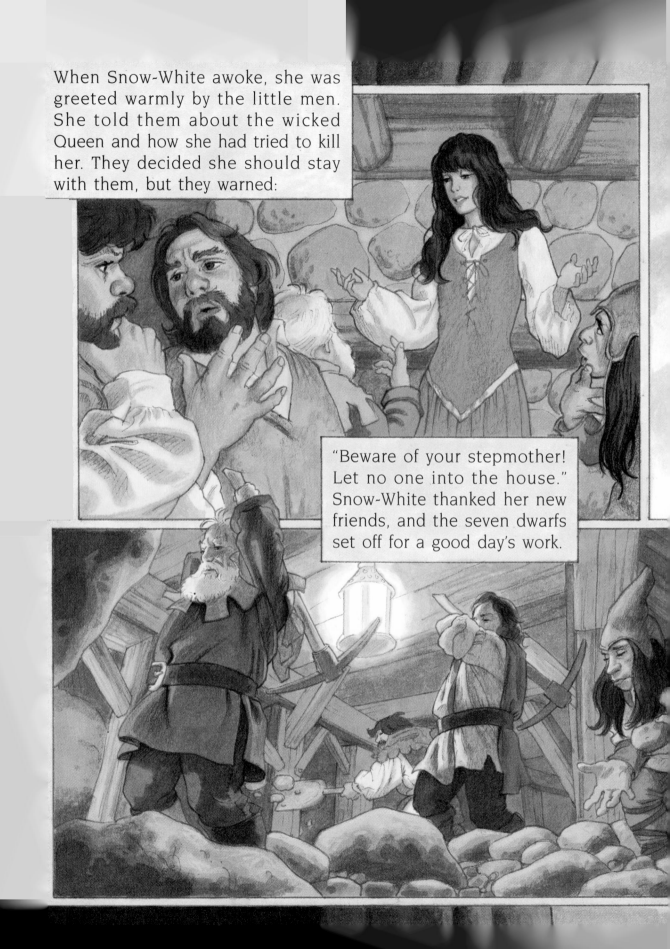

When Snow-White awoke, she was greeted warmly by the little men. She told them about the wicked Queen and how she had tried to kill her. They decided she should stay with them, but they warned:

"Beware of your stepmother! Let no one into the house." Snow-White thanked her new friends, and the seven dwarfs set off for a good day's work.

Thinking Snow-White dead, the Queen vainly stepped up to her mirror, and said, "Mirror, mirror, on the wall,/Who is the fairest of them all?"
And the mirror said, "Queen, you are a beauty rare,/But Snow-White living in the glen/With the seven little men/Is a thousand times more fair."

The Queen tore at her hair, crying, "No! She lives! She lives!" After a time, she said, "I shall kill her myself! By black arts I will undo this child!" And with witchcraft she made a poison apple.

She dressed as an old beggar woman and went to the dwarfs' house. She called, "My dear, I was passing by and heard your sweet singing. I have picked some sweet apples, won't you have one?"

No sooner did Snow-White bite into the apple, than she fell as if dead. But she was not dead.

The apple didn't kill her, but put her into a deep sleep from which nothing the dwarfs did would wake her. In sorrow, the dwarfs placed her in a glass case, that they could watch over her as they prayed and waited. Then one day, a prince rode by.

The young prince fell in love at once with the sleeping maiden. He begged the dwarfs but one little kiss from her sweet lips. Bending down, he gently kissed Snow-White, and the evil spell was broken. She awoke, smiling.

He asked her hand in marriage and Snow-White accepted. He took her away to his kingdom. As for the Queen, she stood in front of her mirror, crying. She grew old, died, and fell to dust.

The Elves and the Shoemaker

There was once a shoemaker who was so poor that he had only enough leather left for one pair of shoes. He cut the leather out late one night and intended to finish his work in the morning. Having done so, he said his prayers, and laid down to sleep.

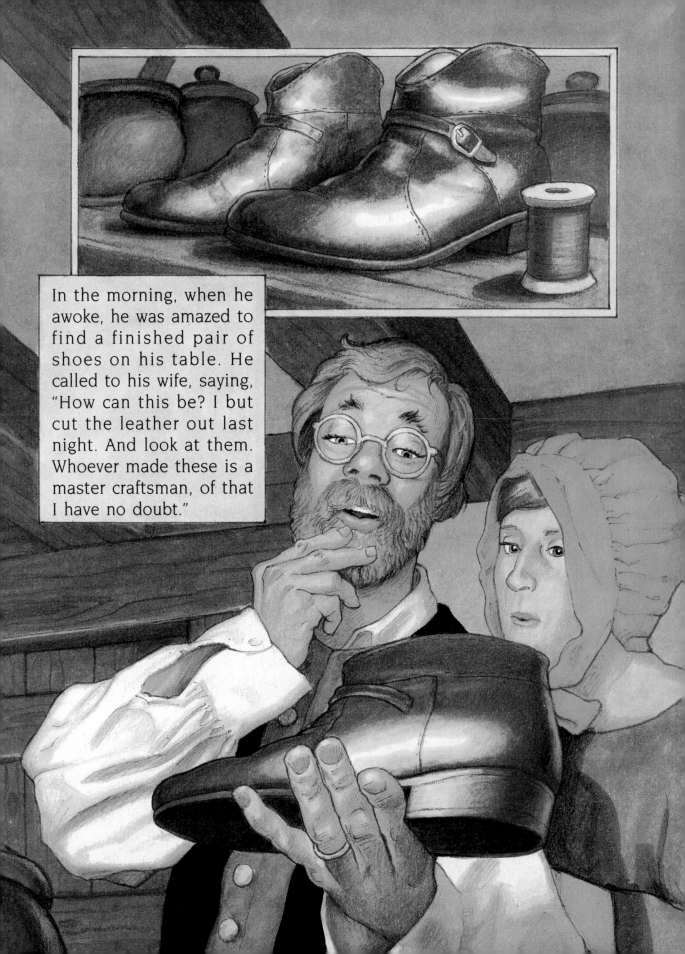

In the morning, when he awoke, he was amazed to find a finished pair of shoes on his table. He called to his wife, saying, "How can this be? I but cut the leather out last night. And look at them. Whoever made these is a master craftsman, of that I have no doubt."

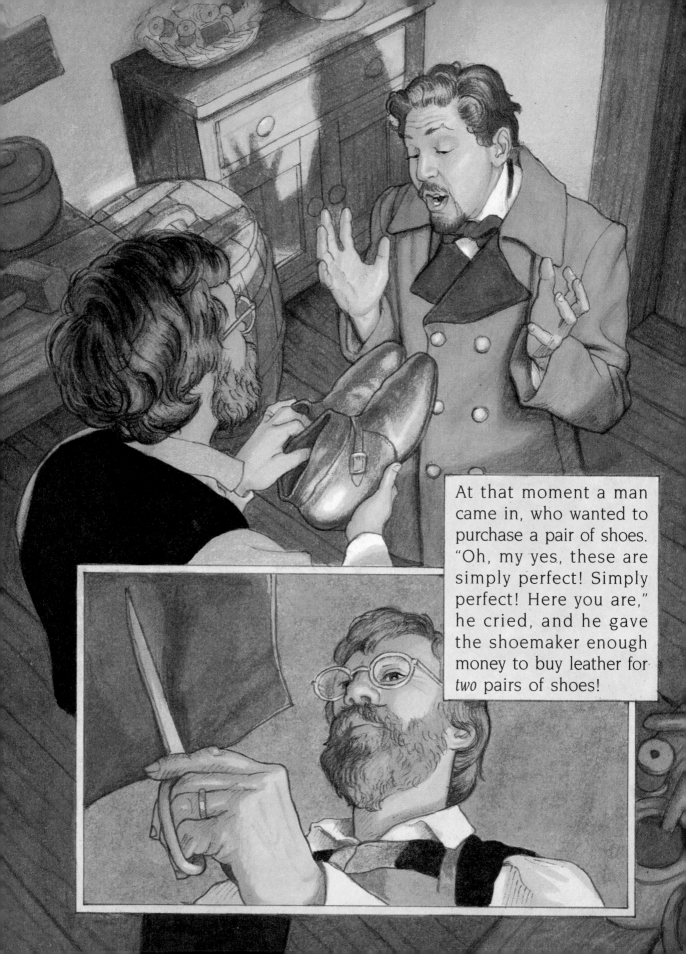

At that moment a man came in, who wanted to purchase a pair of shoes. "Oh, my yes, these are simply perfect! Simply perfect! Here you are," he cried, and he gave the shoemaker enough money to buy leather for *two* pairs of shoes!

He was going to make the shoes the next day, but again when he awoke he found the shoes had already been made.

And he had no lack of customers. From that time on, the shoemaker would cut the leather at night and awake to finished shoes in the morning. Before long, he was quite wealthy.

Now one evening, just before Christmas, he said to his wife, "Why don't we stay up late and hide to see who is giving us all this help." They hid in a corner of the room and waited. At midnight there came two little men through the window.

They were naked, except for tiny green leaves around their waists. They stopped to look and listen, and then they jumped on the table.

They went to work at once, and began to stitch, sew, and hammer the shoes together so quickly that the shoemaker could not believe his eyes! Then they ran swiftly away.

After they had gone, his wife said, "Oh, the poor darlings! They must have clothes! I shall make them little suits."

From leather she made them each a little cap, suit, and shoes. When they came the next night they found the charming clothes, and cried with joy. Quick as could be, they put them on.

Then, dressed in their pretty clothes, they danced, and sang, "Now we're boys so fine and neat,/Why make shoes for other's feet!" And they jumped out the window. They never came back again, but the shoemaker gave thanks every night for all they had done.

The Frog Prince

Long ago there was a King's daughter, a beautiful child, who loved to play with her ball down by a pond. Now it happened one day that the ball fell in the water and sank to the bottom.

She began to weep, for she could never reach it herself. Then she heard a voice, saying, "Why do you weep, my Princess?" It was an ugly Frog.

"I weep because my golden ball has fallen into the pond and I cannot reach it," she said.
"Oh, do not cry," said the Frog. "I can get your ball. What will the King's daughter give me if I do?"
"Anything you wish, dear Frog."

"If you will love me and be my playmate, let me eat from your plate and drink from your cup, and let me sleep in your bed—I shall get your ball." The Princess promised, and the Frog went down for her ball.

The Frog came up again with the ball in his mouth. The Princess took it and started off for the castle. "Wait! Wait! I cannot hop that fast!" But the Princess ran away.

That night a knock came at the castle door, and a voice could be heard, saying. "You promised me, Princess. Now come and let me in!"
Going to the door, she found the Frog waiting outside.
"Go away, you *horrid* Frog!"

But her father, the King, called out to his daughter, saying, "Come here, my child, and tell me what this is all about. Who is at the door?"

And the Princess told her father how she had lost her ball, and that she promised a Frog she would be his friend and companion if he would only swim down and get it for her.

"That which you promise you *must* keep," said the King. "Go, and let the Frog in."

She did as her father commanded, and the Frog followed her to the dining room. "Lift me up," said the Frog, "that I may sit with you."

"Now move your golden plate near me, that I may eat with you." She did so, but turned away in disgust to see him eat. The Frog, however, ate heartily and took no notice.

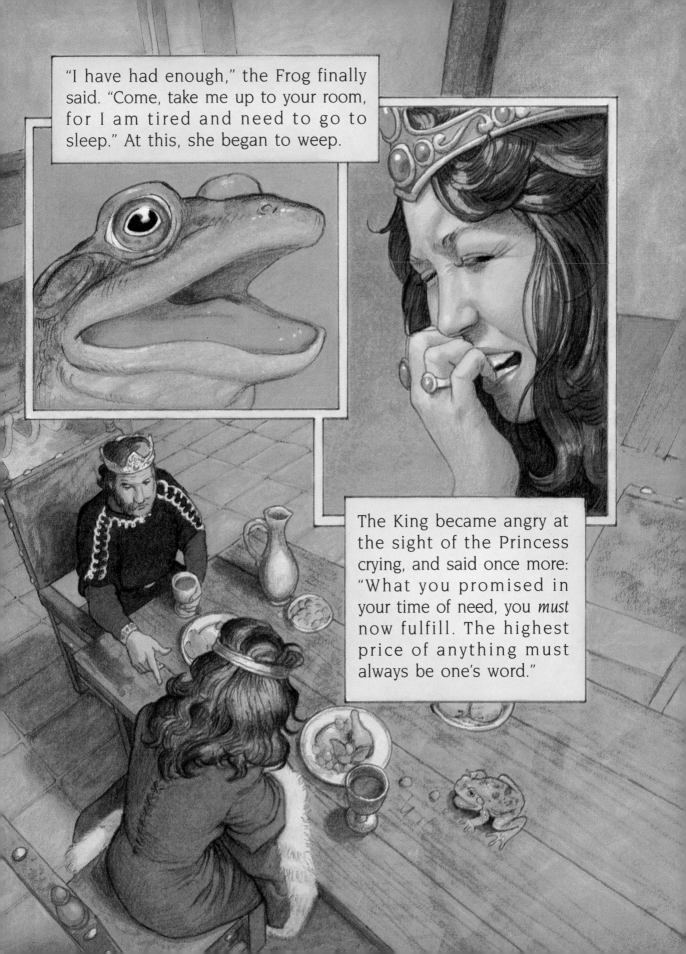

She dried her tears, and picked the Frog up with her finger and thumb, and carried him to her room. Once there, she placed him on the floor.

"I am as tired as you. Pick me up and place me on your little bed that I may sleep. If you don't, I shall tell your father you can't keep a promise." She began to weep softly once again, but she started to do as the Frog asked.

The Frog, seeing she would keep her word, said, "My princess, you do not have to place me on your clean bed. You have kept your word to me. And I am *not* what I seem to be."

And suddenly the Frog turned into a handsome and noble Prince. "Forgive me, Princess, for this poor trick. From first I saw you, I fell in love. But I had to know if you could be true to your word in both heart and deed. I had a wizard transform me into the Frog. I wish your hand in marriage, if you'll have me, and I promise no tricks."

The Princess accepted, and they were married soon after. And the Prince was as true to his word as the Princess was, and together, they lived a very long and happy life.

hansel and Gretel

Deep in a forest there lived a woodcutter with his wife and two children. He named his son Hansel and his daughter Gretel. There had been a famine in the land, and he no longer had any food to feed his family. One night, his wife said, "Tomorrow, we will take the children far into the forest, give them some bread, and leave them there."

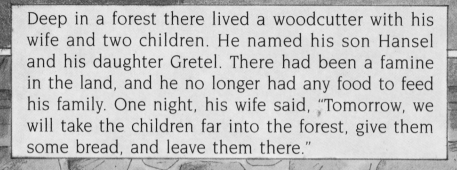

"Leave *my* children! How could I? I won't!" he cried. "You *will*, husband, or we shall all starve! They will find a kinder death in the forest!"

Now Hansel and Gretel were still awake and heard the terrible fate awaiting them in the morning. But Hansel had a plan. He told Gretel: "Don't worry, for as father takes us into the forest, I will drop crumbs of bread along the way. We can return back home by following the crumbs along the path after they've gone. Why, I bet we can be back home before they are!"

In the morning, the wife woke them, saying, "Here, children, take this bread for your supper today. We must go deep into the forest to gather good wood and we want you to come along with us. Hurry now, we have a long way to go before the day is done." And the family set off into the deep woods.

As they walked along, Hansel would drop a crumb of bread behind him from time to time when he was sure his father wasn't watching. They walked all day into the deep, deep wood.

Evening finally came, and their
father said they should stop. He
wanted so to bring his children
back home with him, but he
knew his wife would not stand
for it. He said sadly, "Children, I
have to go farther off to gather
wood. I will make you a nice fire,
and you can stay here." And with
a tear, he left the children alone.

Later that evening, the children set off along the path, following the bread crumbs that Hansel had thrown down. But they hadn't gone far when the bread crumbs just disappeared. Sadly, during the day a thousand birds had swooped down to feed on the bread. They were now lost in the dark forest. Not knowing where to go, they decided to lay down and sleep for the night.

In the morning, they began walking to try to find a way out. Deep in the wood, they came upon a cottage—and the roof was made of gingerbread!

Hansel and Gretel could hardly believe their eyes! They ran to the house, for they hadn't eaten in two days, and began pulling great chunks of ginger-bread from the roof.

No sooner were they stuffing their mouths full of tasty gingerbread, than a voice came from behind, saying, "Nibbling, nibbling like a mouse,/Who's that nibbling the gingerbread house?" Looking up, the children saw an old woman at the door, and they both dropped their food in fright.

"Don't be frightened, children," she said. "Ah, my dears, what has brought you here. Come in, and I will feed you. Come in."

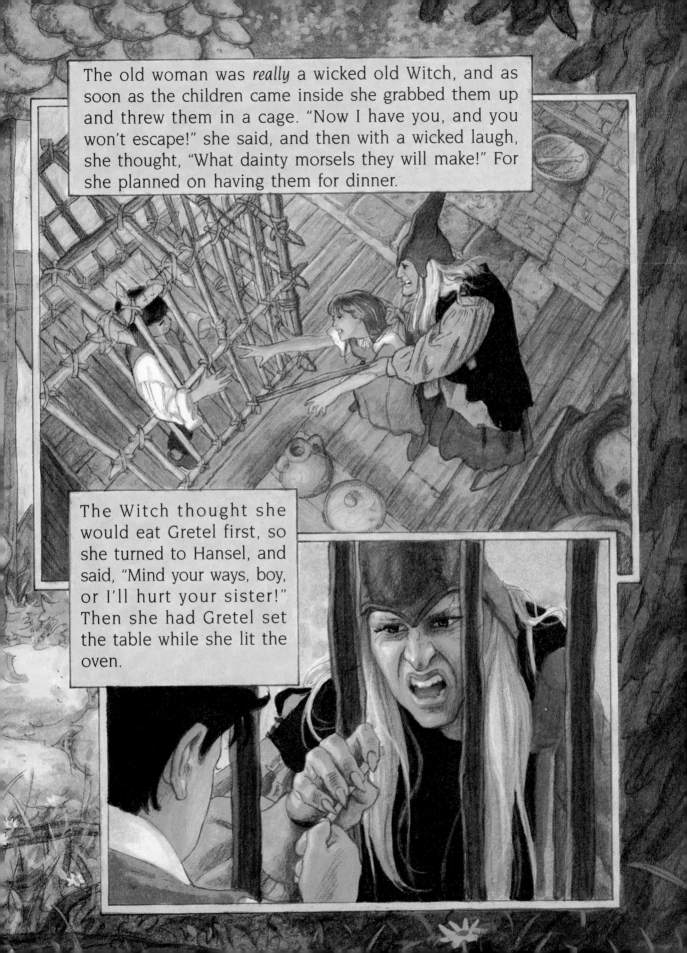

The old woman was *really* a wicked old Witch, and as soon as the children came inside she grabbed them up and threw them in a cage. "Now I have you, and you won't escape!" she said, and then with a wicked laugh, she thought, "What dainty morsels they will make!" For she planned on having them for dinner.

The Witch thought she would eat Gretel first, so she turned to Hansel, and said, "Mind your ways, boy, or I'll hurt your sister!" Then she had Gretel set the table while she lit the oven.

"Go, child, into the oven and fetch me that pan in the back," the Witch told her. "Be quick!"
"But I don't know how to get in?" Gretel cried.
"See here, it's easy!" And as the Witch bent down, Gretel pushed her in.

The Witch was dead. Gretel freed Hansel, and the two ran from the cottage and into the woods. After two days, they found their way home. Their father hugged them, and said, "Oh, forgive me, children! I promise never to send you away again. We will be together forever."